S0-DXO-931
Volume 6

Stories with Holes™

By Nathan Levy

MIND MOTION™

TREND enterprises, Inc.

Stories with Holes Volume 6
©2000 by TREND enterprises, Inc.
Stories with Holes™ and MindMotion™ are trademarks
of TREND enterprises, Inc.

Printed in the United States of America

Juli A. Gordon, editor
Steven Hauge, designer

Library of Congress Catalog Card Number: 99-69753

ISBN 1-889319-54-6

10 9 8 7 6 5 4 3 2

Introduction

Stories with Holes™ challenges participants to creatively use their intelligence to solve intriguing puzzles.

As you "play" Stories with Holes™ you will accomplish these objectives:

- provide growth in imagination and intuitive functioning;

- encourage divergent thinking;

- give experiences that display the fun of working cooperatively, rather than competitively, on a common problem;

- increase cognitive skills of resolving discrepancies through successful experiences;

- provide an enjoyable change of pace for task-oriented learning environments.

This is a structured activity. It is designed to ensure involvement on the part of each participant, while it promotes feelings of group and individual success.

The stories are designed to accommodate age levels from 8 to 88 and all groups—regardless of background, or achievement level.

The time the stories take will vary. Usually, they will take from three to twenty minutes, but some stories can take hours.

Methodology

The first time a group is introduced to Stories with Holes™, it will be necessary to give students the following information. *"I am going to tell you a story with a hole in it—I mean that an important part of the story is missing. Listen carefully so you can find the missing part. The story may not seem to make much sense to you at first..."*

At this point, tell the story once, pause, then tell it exactly the same way again. Then give this next set of directions. *"You can ask questions that can be answered either with a 'yes,' or a 'no'. If I answer 'does not compute,' or 'is not relevant,' that means that the question you asked cannot receive a straight yes or no answer without throwing you off track."*

You can allow for questions about the process, but usually it is best to jump into the game by having the questioning start. The process becomes clear as the game progresses. Once a group has done one story, the full directions will not need to be given again, although students may need to be reminded of some of the rules while playing.

The following is an example of how a story may play out in your classroom:

Leader: Brad lives on the 20th floor of an apartment building. Every time he leaves, he rides an elevator from the 20th floor to the street level. Every time he returns, he rides the same elevator to the 15th floor, where he leaves the elevator and walks up the remaining five flights of stairs. Why?

Player: Does Brad want exercise?

Leader: No.

Player: Does the elevator work right?

Leader: Yes.

Player: Does he have a friend on the 15th floor?

Leader: No.

Player: Where does he go when he leaves the apartment?

Leader: Does not compute.

Player: Does Brad go to work when he leaves the building?

Leader: No.

Player: Is Brad a grownup?

Leader: No. Do you think you know the answer?

Player: Yes.

Leader: Stand up. (Having the student stand allows him or her to be the star and be recognized by everyone in the group.) Why didn't Brad ride the elevator all the way up to the 20th floor?

Player: Brad is a child and can't reach the button for the 20th floor. He can only reach the 15th floor button, so he has to walk the rest of the way.

When a student arrives at the answer, make certain that all participants understand it and why it is correct. Then, instead of starting a new game, particularly if this is the first time this group is playing, spend some time processing the game. Ask questions such as these:

1. What did you have to do to play this game? (*Listen to questions and answers, think, imagine, visualize, follow a line of reasoning, eliminate possibilities, etc.*)

2. When you solved the riddle, did you have any help from others? (*Nearly always the person relied on previous questions and answers. The interdependence of players reduces competition to be "the winner."*)

3. Do you think you could use this type of thinking at other times, besides when we do Stories with Holes™?

Usually a group will be eager to try a second game right away. Generally it is best to wait, and string games out, as a series, over several weeks or months. It might be advisable to "play" a second game right away when the story is solved in a minute or less—too soon for the group to get into the process.

Helpful Hints

1. **After telling a story,** and before the questioning begins, ask if anyone has heard it before and knows the answer. Tell these people to refrain from questioning and only to observe this time.

2. **If a question is impossible** to answer with yes or no, respond by saying "does not compute" or "is not relevant." Watch for these types of questions:

   - Any question that begins with why, where, who, when, what, or which.

   - Questions that assume information that was not given in the story.

   - Irrelevant questions that, if answered, would cause confusion. In this situation, "does not compute, and is not relevant" are answers designed to help the players, not confuse them.

3. **To help the players,** you may periodically use body language or voice inflection. If a player asks something that is not correct but is important for the solution, answer the question in a way that helps the group know to stay on the topic. Smiles, widened eyes, and leaning forward help keep motivation high.

4. **Don't let the game lag.** If the players question for more than 10 to 12 minutes and are not getting anywhere, try one of these options:

- Review important information that has already been learned. You may want to include a suggestion of where to focus questions. (For example, we've established that the elevator is working correctly, but we really don't know anything about Brad as a person.) If you feel that a story is too difficult, ask or answer leading questions that they may not have thought about.

- Invite individuals who have already heard the story to ask leading questions that hint at the answer, but that do not give away the story's final solution.

- There is nothing wrong with leaving the story unsolved. The group can return to it another time, when interest and energy are high. Some students may protest, but do not give the answer. The experience of non-closure has some valuable learning in itself; but more importantly, once a group has worked hard on a story, the victory should be an earned one.

5. **Share the role of leader.** When the group is familiar with the process that you have modeled, have a volunteer read the story and field questions. Pass the leadership role around. From the outset, stress that the role of the leader is to be helpful; it is not to frustrate the group.

6. **Encourage categorical thinking.** When a player asks a question beginning with "Would it help us to know…" or "Does it have anything to do with…" pause the game to show how this type of question narrows the range of questions. It helps focus the group's attention towards important information and helps avoid irrelevant questions. For example, the question, "Is the person's occupation important?" is more useful than, "Is he a plumber?"

7. **Be sure that a question is exactly true,** or exactly false, before responding. One word in a question can make the difference. If a player asks, "Is the man stopping on the 15th floor because he wants excercise?" the answer would be "Does not compute," because "man" is an assumption.

The Teacher's Order

The teacher's order was ignored.
She was very pleased.
Why?

Answer:

The teacher ordered an inexpensive steak at a restaurant. The owner of the restaurant was a former student of the teacher's, and he made sure she received the very best steak on the menu.

❓ The Runners

Through the heat they ran and ran, day and night for 40 days straight. They took no breaks for meals, drinks, or sleep. The only thing that finally stopped them was the extreme cold weather that came about. How could this be?

➔ Ⓐnswer:

Noses ran because of allergy season. A frost finally stopped the allergies.

10

Bald Bill

Though he was bald, Bill brushed his hare every day. No one ever made fun of him, and he did not wear a wig.
Why?

Answer:

The hare Bill brushed was his pet rabbit.

❓ Mark the Pitcher

Mark, a little league pitcher, took his time as he prepared for the last inning of the game. He walked slowly toward the mound. When he got there, he realized that the mound was gone! No official stopped the game. Mark pitched the last inning anyway.

What had happened?

Answer:

The "mound" in this case was a candy bar Mark was going to eat. One of his teammates had eaten it.

Lori's Barrel

Lori's barrel weighed 60 pounds. Lori put a few things in the barrel that made it weigh less. How is this possible?

Answer:

Lori put holes in the barrel. Water ran out of the holes causing the barrel to weigh less.

13

❓ Mr. Long's New Suit

Mr. Long put on his new suit and went to work. While at work, Mr. Long tore his suit slightly. His partners were unable to work with Mr. Long looking the way he did. Why?

➔ Ⓐnswer:

Mr. Long was a scuba diver. When a rock punctured his scuba suit, water rushed in and he had to return to the surface. His partners needed him for the project they were working on underwater; therefore, all of the divers had to return to the surface with him.

Eileen's Sister

Eileen's 10-year-old sister Kim drove her there, annoying Eileen all the way.
How could this be?

Answer:

Eileen's sister had driven her up the wall.

Mary and the Castle Keys

Mary reached down and touched the castle's antique keys even though the sign said "Do Not Touch!" The security guards came running, along with many others. Mary continued to touch the keys and no one tried to stop her. Why?

Answer:

Mary was a concert pianist. The owner of the antique piano had asked her to play it at a party he was throwing in his castle. Every one came running to hear Mary play.

Laura and the Wild Flowers

Laura loved to pick wild flowers. One day she wandered deep into the forest where she saw the largest and most beautiful "dandy" lion of them all. She didn't pick this one though. Why?

Answer:

This was a real "dandy" lion that had escaped from the zoo.

17

❓ Touchdown!

Neil and Ed worked together to make a beautiful touchdown. The people watching roared and cheered when it was made. The game plan was followed and all rules abided by, yet no points were awarded.
Why?

Ⓐnswer:

Neil Armstrong and Edwin Aldrin Jr., were the first two people to land on the moon. They touched down on July 20, 1969.

18

Ryan and the Giant

Last year when Ryan saw the Giant coming toward him, he was not afraid. This year when he saw the Giant coming, he started to run away—even though he was still not afraid. Why?

Answer:

Ryan played for the Giants football team last year. This year, Ryan was on a different team. The Giant coming towards him this year was trying to tackle him.

? Jennifer's Boyfriend

Jennifer's boyfriend had a new sports car and was to pick her up after work to show it to her. While she waited, it started to rain. She had no umbrella, no raincoat, and no hat, yet, when her boyfriend finally came 15 minutes later, she got into the car perfectly dry. How is this possible?

Answer:

Jennifer was waiting inside.

20

Young Glen

Glen was upset. None of the young people on the crowded bus had offered to stand so that an older woman with her arms full of packages could sit. Glen wouldn't offer his seat; even though, he was as strong and healthy as all the others. Why?

Answer:

Glen was the bus driver.

❓ The Baseball Game

Two entire baseball teams were there, but they couldn't play. Neither team owner was upset.
Why?

Ⓐnswer:

Two children were showing each other their baseball cards. Each had a complete team.

22

Silly Millie

Millie is silly, but not ridiculous. She's funny and sorry, but not humorous or apologetic. She eats apples, but not pears. She'll attend a rally, but not a party. She'll cut with scissors, but not with a knife. Why?

Answer:

Millie only likes things that have double consonants.

? The Hotel Dog

Jack registered at the Hotel El
Perro. The owner of the hotel
was seated with a friendly
looking poodle. "Does your
dog bite?" asked Jack. "No,"
said the proprietor. So Jack
leaned over to pet the dog,
and the dog bit him.
What happened?

Answer:

The poodle did not belong
to the proprietor. The
proprietor's dog, a cocker
spaniel, does not bite.

The Horse

The horse had never been fed or groomed by the owner, yet it continued to work well. Why?

Answer:

The "horse" was a sawhorse in a woodworker's shed.

Crossing the River

A man wanted to row across a river with his pet weasel, a rooster, and some corn. His boat was so small that he could only carry one item at a time. To complicate the problem, the weasel, if left alone, would eat the rooster, and the rooster would eat the corn. How did he cross the river with his possessions intact?

Answer:

The man took the rooster to the other side first, then rowed back to get the weasel. He rowed the weasel across, left it on the other side, but brought the rooster back. Then he brought the corn across, rowed back, and brought the rooster across again.

27

❓ The All-Night Market

Ingrid, who is always quick to panic, went food shopping in an all-night market and parked her car in a distant part of the parking lot. As she completed her shopping, all the electricity in the market went off. The emergency parking lights were not on and she didn't have a flashlight. She calmly and quickly located her car.
How did she do it?

28

Answer:

It was early afternoon when she finished shopping. She didn't need any lights because it was during the day.

!

29

Behind Bars

Ken and Chris spent the major part of their lives behind bars. Neither of them had ever committed a crime. What happened?

Answer:

Ken and Chris were two-year-old twins. They were often put in a playpen together.